I pretend that I can fly.
I zoom through the clouds
High in the sky!

I pretend that I'm a shark
Deep in the ocean
Down where it's dark.

I pretend that I'm on T.V.
I have my own show –
Hey look at me!

I pretend that I can make
Robots that bake
Green tower cakes!

I pretend that I can switch
The world around
With a magic swish!

Birds fly upside down.
Dogs live in trees.
Fish walk on the ground...

We can slide down rainbows

And swing from stars.

We can bounce on clouds

And drive fast cars.

The sky is purple,
The trees are red,
And the grass turned shades of blue.

Water is yellow,
Clouds are green,
And we are orange, too!

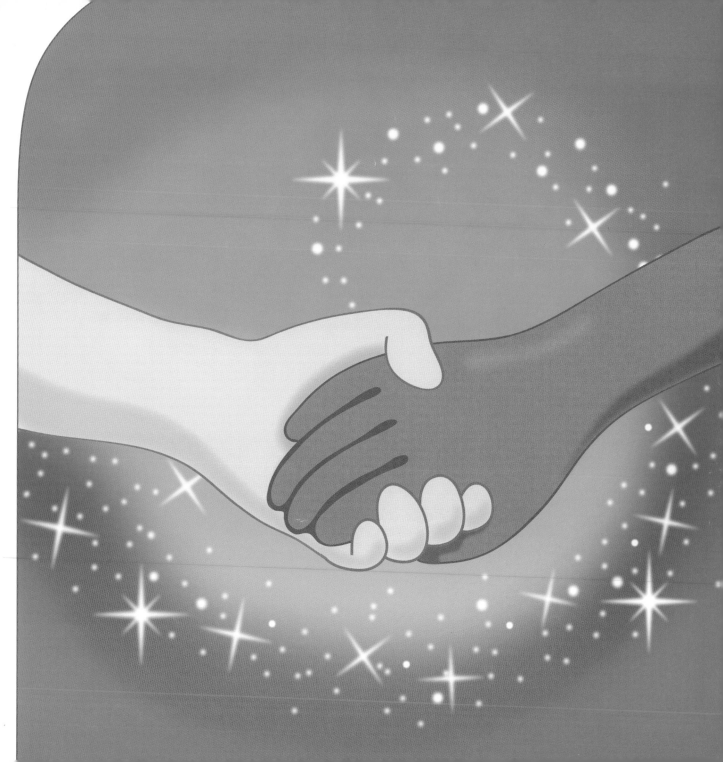

The PUMPKINHEADS ANSWER:

What do you IMAGINE?

Danza:
That I can explore the ocean!

Sage:
That I make people laugh!

Ella: That I invent useful (and fun) things.

Lulu:
That sometimes everything changes colors, including people!

Xavy:

That I'm a
superhero and
I help people!

Carmin:

That everyone in
the world takes
care of each other!

Cameron:

That I'm a
sports star.

A Message from the Pumpkinheads:

Imagine and dream. Play and learn.
Now **you** have the wand. It is your turn.
What will you change? Who will you be?
Anything's possible - try it and see!

KEEP DREAMING!

www.pumpkinheads.com

Spark your Imagination!

1. Draw your own silly world! Change anything you want (for example, colors, where animals live, how things grow). We don't want to give you too many hints - use your imagination!
2. Tell your own story! Who is in your story, what is happening in the story, how does it end?
3. Create your own game! How many players are there? What happens when you win? Anything is possible!
4. What is one thing you would change to improve the world? How can you help make this change?

Pumpkinheads award-winning books focus on social and emotional development. Our series aims to help our little ones build awareness of their feelings, along with learning from and interacting with others. We believe it is never too early to learn character developing concepts, especially through fun and relatable characters. Above all, we believe in *Learning Through Play!*

Don't miss out on more Pumpkinheads adventures!

Karen Kilpatrick

Karen, mom, attorney and award-winning author, has been writing and creating for as long as she can remember. Her passion for entertaining and teaching young children led her to create Pumpkinheads – the book series that focuses on social and emotional development for young children. She believes that qualities such as courage, kindness, tolerance, and appreciation can be taught and that it's never too early to learn character-building concepts, especially from fun books! She lives in Florida with her son and two daughters.

Tara Louise Campbell

As soon as Tara could hold a crayon in her hand, her endless journey with art began. From art classes at an early age to a Bachelor of Arts in Fine Art, Tara's love for art has never subsided. After college, she spent 15 years as a digital artist. During this time, Tara started her own company, Sunshine Creative Studios, as an outlet for expressing her passion for creating children's art. To see Tara's latest work, please visit www.taralouisecampbell.com.

Matthew Wilson

Matthew's career in animation began in early 1991, at the age of 17. He was taken under the personal direction of the classic Walt Disney trained animator, John Ewing, who was himself trained by the "Nine Old Men of Disney." He gained a solid foundation in the classic traditions passed down by the forefathers of the art. Matthew has worked as an animator on both Warner Brothers and Disney TV series, such as Steven Spielberg's Tiny Toons and Animaniacs, Disney's Timon and Pumbaa, Hercules and Duck Daze to name a few.